Disney's
Winnie the Pooh's
HALLOWEEN

By Bruce Talkington

DISNEY PRESS

NEW YORK

**Illustrations by Vaccaro Associates, Inc.
Layout by Ennis McNulty
Painted by Lou Paleno**

1   3   5   7   9   10   8   6   4   2

Library of Congress Catalog Card Number: 93-70934
ISBN: 1-56282-540-2

The late afternoon sun appeared to hesitate on the horizon, settling comfortably among the tip-top branches of the trees of the Hundred-Acre Wood as if reluctant to turn off its light and make way for the night.

"Look," chuckled Winnie the Pooh from the grassy knoll where he and his friends were watching the sunset. "The sun doesn't want to go to bed!"

"Perhaps it's afraid of the dark," suggested Piglet, who was much fonder of the sun's arriving and spending the day than he was of its going to bed and leaving animals to bump around in the dark and bruise their very small shins and noses and upset their delicate nerves.

Christopher Robin put his arm comfortingly around Piglet's shoulders. "No, Piglet," he explained, "the sun simply wants to stay and share Halloween with us."

"Oh?" remarked Pooh Bear, his tummy rumbling with sudden interest. "Is Halloween, perhaps, a very small smackeral of something sweet —," he licked his lips hopefully, "—to eat?"

"Don't be silly, Pooh Bear," snorted Rabbit. "A Halloween isn't something to eat."

"'Course not," agreed Tigger, bouncing up and down on his coiled tail. "Everybody knows that."

"Pardon me for saying so," interrupted Eeyore, looking up from where he was sniffing a particularly tasty-looking thistle, "but knowing what something isn't doesn't exactly tell us what something is, which seems to me to be the point, if that's what we're looking for. The point, I mean."

"Never mind the point," whistled Gopher. "All I want to know is what the ding-dang we're talking about!"

"Halloween," announced Pooh, proud of himself for remembering.

"And what exactly *is* a Halloween?" demanded Gopher.

The friends exchanged shrugs and puzzled frowns, then turned to Christopher Robin for an answer.

Pooh smiled. Christopher Robin always had answers for the confusing questions that found their way to the Hundred-Acre Wood.

"Halloween," Christopher Robin informed them excitedly, "is the scariest holiday of the year — because it takes place at night."

"You mean," gulped Piglet, "it's a holi-*day* that takes place in the very dark darkness?"

"The darker the better, Piglet. Things are so much more frightening then, don't you think?"

"If you don't mind," responded Piglet, trying to keep his ears from trembling, "I think I'll be thinking as little as possible about scary things that happen in the dark."

"But that's what Halloween is," protested Christopher Robin. "When the sun goes down, we all dress up in costumes and see who can be the scariest."

Piglet noticed the sun was no longer resting comfortably in the treetops but was, in fact, almost out of sight behind the horizon, one last bright gleam peeping over the rim of the earth.

"Uh, I'm sorry, but I won't have time to play Halloween with you," Piglet blurted out. "I have some very important things to do."

"What could be more important than scaring the pants off each other in the dark?" Tigger wanted to know.

"Turning on every light in my house and dusting under my bed," said Piglet.

"But Piglet," asked Pooh, "who cares whether or not there's dust under your bed?"

"I do," answered Piglet, hurrying away into the dusk, "because that's where I'm going to be spending Halloween!"

"Poor Piglet," sighed Christopher Robin. "But I suppose the nice thing about a holiday is that we all have the opportunity to suit ourselves."

"And that's just what I'm going to do," laughed Tigger, bouncing around his friends in excited circles. "Suit myself up in the most fantastical costume I can think of! Hoo-hoo-HOO!"

As the others shouted their agreement, Pooh was strangely silent.

"What's the matter, Pooh Bear?" Christopher Robin asked as they all scattered to their homes to prepare their costumes.

"Well," Pooh responded, thoughtfully scratching an ear, "I suppose I'm going to miss sharing Halloween with my best friend, Piglet."

"That is too bad," Christopher Robin agreed. "You're simply going to have to have twice as much fun as anyone else and share it with him later."

"Why, what a nice idea!" exclaimed Pooh. "And I'll have to be twice as scary, too."

"You'd better get started on your costume," laughed Christopher Robin.

"Oh yes," Pooh mused, beginning a slow ramble home. "My costume."

Pooh remembered that his scariest experiences were whenever he visited the honey tree for an extra smackeral or two (or more!) before, or after, whatever meal it happened to be. (Eating always made Pooh very hungry.)

"Nothing is scarier than a honey-bee," Pooh decided, "and that's what I'm going to be...a BEE!"

So when Pooh arrived home, he immediately opened up his chest of odds, ends, and middles of items of no possible use to anyone except to a bear of very little brain and began to look for his costume.

In no time at all Pooh was ready.

With black paint, Pooh had painted large stripes around his middle.

A plunger was stuck to his sitting-down side (with a small pennant attached proclaiming Stinger in case anyone needed reminding).

And on his head were Pooh's answer to antennae, two wobbly springs capped with Ping-Pong balls.

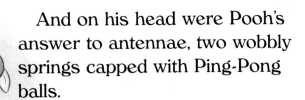

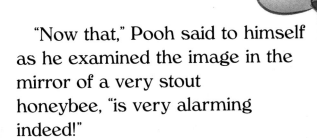

"Now that," Pooh said to himself as he examined the image in the mirror of a very stout honeybee, "is very alarming indeed!"

He hurried out to meet his friends, convinced there would be no one better suited for Halloween than he!

The night had become quite dark despite a sky full of stars and a huge autumn moon. Pooh would have walked right over Gopher without seeing him, but then he noticed two glowing eyes peering out of the gloom.

"Well?" Gopher's voice demanded. "What do you think?"

Pooh had to look very closely to distinguish his practically invisible friend at all! He was wrapped head to foot in a billowing black cloak.

"Gopher!" Pooh exclaimed, quite startled by his friend's sudden appearance. "You certainly surprised me!"

"I knew I would," Gopher snickered, tugging the black cloth more tightly around himself. "Nothing's spookier than a dark night, so that's what I decided to be. Scared myself out of a week's sleep when I looked in the mirror. Love this Halloween."

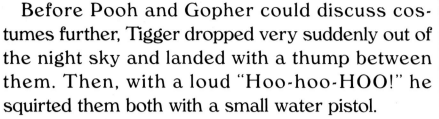

Before Pooh and Gopher could discuss costumes further, Tigger dropped very suddenly out of the night sky and landed with a thump between them. Then, with a loud "Hoo-hoo-HOO!" he squirted them both with a small water pistol.

"Tigger," spluttered Pooh, rubbing the water out of his eyes and gazing at his friend in wonder.

Tigger had donned a bright red jersey with a wriggly bolt of yellow lightning emblazoned across the front.

"Who do you think you are?" whistled Gopher as he wiped his face with the corner of his cloak.

"You know the rainstorm everyone's so afraid is going to show up at the wrong time and rain on whatever it is they don't want rained on?" Tigger gave Gopher and Pooh another little squirt each. "Well, I'm here! Terrifryin', ain't I?"

"Not to me," rumbled a voice from behind them.

All three spun around in surprise. "Eeyore!" they shouted with delight.

Eeyore was wearing a large red nose carefully taped over his own as well as a yellow ruffled collar around his neck. On his head was perched the tallest and pointiest clown hat anyone had ever seen. And it was crowned by a huge, feathery orange ball.

"I was afraid if I were too frightening, I'd have to spend Halloween alone," Eeyore explained. "Hope I didn't frighten anyone too badly."

"Just barely, Eeyore," Pooh reassured him. "If I hadn't heard your friendly voice first, I'm sure I would be running for my life this very moment."

"No doubt about it," added Gopher.

"Abso-posilutely," agreed Tigger.

"I shouldn't believe you for a minute," grumbled Eeyore. Then a smile spread over his face. "But I'm going to because it feels so good."

The four friends began a long, loud laugh that stopped very suddenly in the middle when they saw Rabbit staring at them in annoyance.

"What are you laughing at?" Rabbit wanted to know. "This is the most frightening costume I could think of."

Rabbit had pasted soft clumps of white cotton all over himself.

"It's...it's..." They all struggled for a suitable word.

"It's...very fluffy!" Pooh finally blurted out.

"Perhaps it would be more frightening," suggested Eeyore gently, "if you told us what you are."

Rabbit leaned close and whispered, "A dust bunny!" and shuddered at the thought. "There's nothing more frightening to me than those little balls of lint with minds of their own collecting where I can't take a broom to them!"

The thought of wayward dust suddenly reminded Pooh of Piglet huddled alone under his bed.

"I'm sure Piglet would be terrified of your costume, Rabbit," said Pooh sadly.

Before Rabbit could respond, however, a long, low moan sounded, rattling ominously out of the darkness, causing everyone to stiffen in surprise.

"Woooooooooooooooooo!"

"What was that?" Tigger whispered.

"I don't think I want to wait to see this costume," said Rabbit with a shiver.

"Me, neither," responded Gopher through chattering teeth.

Another moan drifted out of the blackness under the trees. "Woooooooooooooooooo!"

"I think we should go to Piglet's," suggested Pooh, "and make sure he's not too frightened."

"Woooooooooooooooooo!" The moan sounded much closer this time.

"You're right, Pooh. That's what friends are for. Last one to Piglet's house is...not first!" shouted Tigger.

The friends ran headlong through the Hundred-Acre Wood, silver moonlight illuminating the path beneath their pounding feet.

In the distance Piglet's house had every light ablaze and shone like a beacon to guide weary travelers home.

Tigger threw open Piglet's front door and sped inside, followed closely by Rabbit, Gopher, and Pooh, with a panting Eeyore bringing up the rear.

Thundering across Piglet's gleaming floors, they all tried to stop, but the hours of careful waxing by the fastidious Piglet proved their downfall. Skidding through the house, feet skating frantically for a foothold, they all slipped onto their soft sides and slid in a tangle to end up in a pile under Piglet's bed!

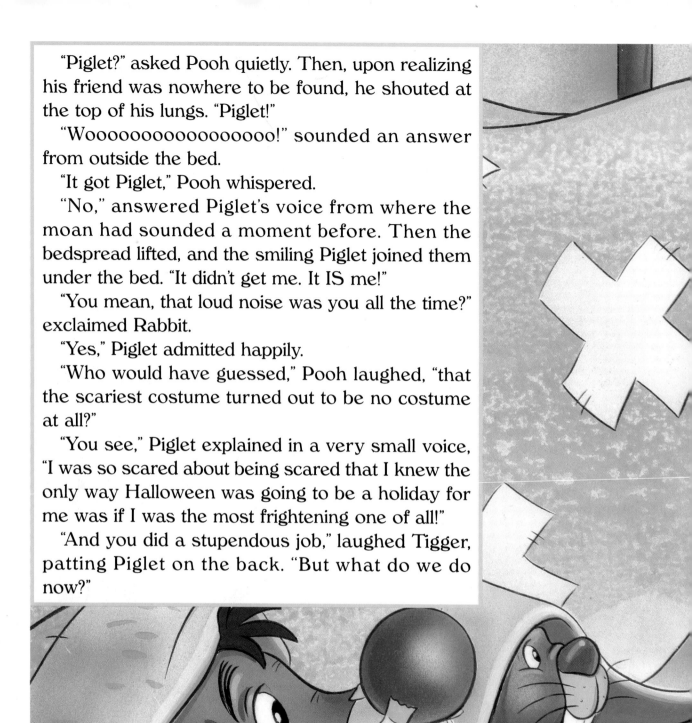

"Piglet?" asked Pooh quietly. Then, upon realizing his friend was nowhere to be found, he shouted at the top of his lungs. "Piglet!"

"Woooooooooooooooooo!" sounded an answer from outside the bed.

"It got Piglet," Pooh whispered.

"No," answered Piglet's voice from where the moan had sounded a moment before. Then the bedspread lifted, and the smiling Piglet joined them under the bed. "It didn't get me. It IS me!"

"You mean, that loud noise was you all the time?" exclaimed Rabbit.

"Yes," Piglet admitted happily.

"Who would have guessed," Pooh laughed, "that the scariest costume turned out to be no costume at all?"

"You see," Piglet explained in a very small voice, "I was so scared about being scared that I knew the only way Halloween was going to be a holiday for me was if I was the most frightening one of all!"

"And you did a stupendous job," laughed Tigger, patting Piglet on the back. "But what do we do now?"

"Well," said Pooh thoughtfully, noting how cozy it was all snuggled together under Piglet's bed. "Why don't we stay here and share Halloween?"

"And have hot chocolate," suggested Eeyore.

"And tell scary stories," added Tigger.

"Excellent!" announced Rabbit. "I'll go first. Once upon a time, there was a giant dust bunny...."

As Rabbit continued, Pooh put his arm around Piglet's shoulders, and they exchanged happy smiles.

"I think I like Halloween, Pooh Bear," Piglet whispered to his friend.

"Me, too, Piglet," Pooh whispered back as he scooted closer. "Me, too!"